Jules-Amédée Barbey d'Aurevilly

Hannibal's Ring

Translated and with an Introduction by

Brian Stableford

THIS IS A SNUGGLY BOOK

ISBN: 978-1-64525-016-6

HANNIBAL'S RING

JULES-AMÉDÉE BARBEY D'AUREVILLY (1808-1889) was born in Normandy into a fervently Royalist and Catholic family. The influence of Byron and other pillars of English and German Romanticism on his early poetry and prose was very marked. In 1845 he wrote *Du dandysme et de George Brummel*, which was followed by several important novels, such as *L'Ensorcelée* (1852) and *Le Chevalier Des Touches* (1863). It was not until 1874, however, that his masterpiece *Les Diaboliques* was released. His work can be seen as a precursor to the Decadent Movement, and was a major influence on many writers, such as Auguste Villiers de l'Isle-Adam and Léon Bloy.

BRIAN STABLEFORD'S scholarly work includes *New Atlantis: A Narrative History of Scientific Romance* (Wildside Press, 2016), *The Plurality of Imaginary Worlds: The Evolution of French roman scientifique* (Black Coat Press, 2017) and *Tales of Enchantment and Disenchantment: A History of Faerie* (Black Coat Press, 2019). In support of the latter projects he has translated more than a hundred volumes of *roman scientifique* and more than twenty volumes of *contes de fées* into English.

His recent fiction, in the genre of metaphysical fantasy, includes a trilogy of novels set in West Wales, consisting of *Spirits of the Vasty Deep* (2018), *The Insubstantial Pageant* (2018) and *The Truths of Darkness* (2019), published by Snuggly Books.

Contents

Introduction

*L*A BAGUE D'ANNIBAL by Jules-Amédée Barbey d'Aurevilly, here translated as *Hannibal's Ring*, was first published in *Le Globe* in 1842 before being reprinted as a book by Duprey in 1843. It had been written some years earlier, begun in December 1834; the assertion contained in a letter the author wrote in 1851 that it was completed in a single night need not be taken seriously. It was not the author's first substantial prose work, having been preceded in its composition by "Le Cachet d'onyx" (written 1831; published 1919) and "Léa" (1832), and it was also preceded into print by the subsequently-penned *Le Amour impossible* (1841; in book form 1843), but it remains the most interesting of his early works because it laid an important foundation-stone for his career, in terms of its subject-matter and its extravagant mannerisms, which established it as a key example of what Théophile Gautier was later to characterize as "Decadent style."

Like the two *nouvelles* that preceded it, *La Bague d'Annibal* seems to have been a product of the infatuations to which the author was subject while living in Caen after finishing his studies in law, in this case with Louise, the wife of Alfred du Méril, his cousin by marriage. Unlike the earlier stories, however, *La Bague d'Annibal* was written during a return to Caen after a reflective absence while resident in Paris, when the infatuation in question was already a thing of the past, a twingeing scar rather than an open wound, and that difference of situation made a considerable contribution to the bitterly jaundiced flavor of the story and helped to secure its importance as a prototype of Decadent prose.

The "Madame" to whom the story is addressed is not a specific object of fervent amorous desire, as the addressee of "Le Cachet d'Onyx" seems to be, but is deliberately distanced and generalized. In 1834 Louise du Méril and the other objects of his temporary amorous obsessions had apparently become, for Barbey, symbols of womankind in general, exemplars of an essential perfidy, which, he had persuaded himself, was common to them all. That was an idea to which he clung with the uncompromising obstinacy that he unhesitatingly attributes as a cardinal character-trait to Aloys, the hero of *La Bague d'Annibal*, whom, he later confessed—not that anyone could possibly have doubted it—was an idealized representation of himself. It was a notion that he repeated insistently and obsessively in his fiction, forming the connecting thread of his most famous work, the story-collection *Les Diaboliques* (withdrawn after its initial publication in 1874 following its prosecution for obscenity; reissued 1883; tr. as *The She-Devils*).

Jules Barbey—the d'Aurevilly was a belated addition inherited from his uncle—was born in Normandy in 1808 into a fervently Royalist and Catholic family, and thus, quite naturally, became a fervent Republican and positivist by way of adolescent rebellion, although that abrupt reaction also paved the way for his eventual equally-abrupt reversion to devout Catholicism, and the evolution of political opinions that were, to say the least, a trifle confused. He began writing poetry in the early 1820s, heavily influenced by his cousin, Edelstand du Méril (1801-1871), a poet and philosopher then besotted with Romanticism and its associated metaphysics, who introduced him to the work of Lord Byron and recruited his assistance in launching the short-lived *Revue de Caen*, in which "Léa" appeared. Byron became and remained Barbey's principal idol and role model, surviving his ideological conversions, although he does not seem to have played a similar role for Edelstand du Méril, who subsequently became a Medievalist of some note.

The influence of Byron and other pillars of English and German Romanticism on Barbey's early poetry and prose is very marked, and it was not restricted to his literary work; his interpretation of the Byronian world-view became the essence of his attitude and his social pose, which he later described as "dandysme." Although that term was widely used simply to identify a dress code, for Barbey and its other major literary popularizers—most notably Honoré de Balzac and Charles Baudelaire—it was a philosophy and a way of life. In his treatise *Du dandysme et de George Brummel* (1845) Barbey describes that philosophy as being born of "an endless struggle between convention and ennui" inescapable in modern aristocratic society, in response to which the dandy deliberately isolates himself mentally from his shallow fellows while continuing to inhabit their society, conceiving of himself metaphorically as a "futile sovereign of a futile world," cultivating a difficult but precious freedom from emotion, a passion for luxury and artificiality, and a calculated "audacity" and "impertinence."

The extent to which Barbey managed to achieve and sustain that pose in real life is dubious, although he was better equipped for it socially than Balzac or Baudelaire, and thus suffered a little less from the resentful chagrin that became hallmarks of their psychological stance. Like them, however, Barbey found the suppression of emotion enormously difficult, because he, like them, was very prone to spontaneous infatuation, and thus perennially at war with himself. In his work, however, he found it easier to construct characters capable of fulfilling his ambitions in their poses, and one of the characters he designed most earnestly and most ambitiously with that end in mind is Aloys in *La Bague d'Annibal*, who thus became a paradigm example of the mind-set of the dandy, allegedly the most perfect heroic product of contemporary social decadence.

Barbey had not yet adopted the term "dandysme" when he wrote the story, so Aloys is categorized as a *fat* [fop] rather than a dandy, but his dandyism is nevertheless not merely recognizable but archetypal. He is an obvious ancestor of many characters invented in a later era by the admirers of Barbey's work who inspired the "Decadent Movement" of the *fin-de-siècle*, prominent among whom were Joris-Karl Huysmans and Jean Lorrain; any attempt to trace the literary ancestry of the former's Jean Des Esseintes in *À rebours* (1884) and the latter's *Monsieur de Phocas* (1900) has to give Aloys a significant place in their genealogy.

Unlike its predecessors, which are tales of unfortunately-doomed love, *La Bague d'Annibal* is not so much a love story as an anti-love story: an account of heroic resistance to the erotic impulse—metaphorically represented in the story as Eve's temptation of Adam—which is orientated toward the possibility of a triumphant escape from the marriage that was already accepted in 1834 as the central component of the conventional ending of modern prose fiction: a crucial defining factor of a "happy ending." As such, *La Bague d'Annibal* is also a war story: an account of an episode in an endless battle being fought in the contemporary salons of French high society, in which the great enemy of the dandy is the horde of womankind—although, as the text of the novelette conscientiously points out, it would be unjust to blame women for their opposition to dandy audacity and impertinence, that opposition being obliged by the social situation imposed upon them by men and tightly bound with ingenious conventional restrictions.

Joséphine, therefore, is as much a product of the decadence of the epoch as Aloys, caught up in the same struggle between convention and ennui, fighting her own battle with an almost-equal expertise. If she is his adversary—perhaps even a "*diabolique*"—it is not because she is inherently evil, but because she has been dealt a bad hand in the game of salon culture, and has no alternative but to play it with all the cunning she can muster. Like Aloys, but in a necessarily different fashion, she is an adherent and extravagant employer of artificiality and luxury, whom he cannot help but admire as well as desire even while disparaging her supposed limitations.

Although Barbey changed his religious and political views drastically in the 1840s, altering the complexion of the impertinence and the audacity that he considered essential components of his dandyism—thus ensuring that his prolific critical writing would win him a great many adversaries and opponents, not to say enemies—one of the most remarkable things about him was that it never threatened the diehard cynicism of his work or made it seem problematic to him. A dandy he was and a dandy he remained to the end, that faith never coming into conflict inside his ingenious mind with the recovered religious faith in the pugnacious absence of which it had initially been developed. To many of his contemporaries that seemed bizarre, and he was widely considered to be a paradoxical character—which he loved, paradoxicality being one of the principal indulgences and weapons of his wit, and of the behavioral challenge that he felt it absolutely necessary to present to the world.

The particular character of Barbey's paradoxicality became obvious for the first time in the personality of Aloys, who is a kind of ideal type thereof, and although it continued to develop thereafter as the fledgling litterateur became a prolific and combative journalist as well as an underrated novelist, it did not change fundamentally. That obstinacy in paradoxicality can be seen, in retrospect, as one of the key features of the Decadent Movement, typical of its practitioners as well as their works. It flowered initially in the work of the most radical members of the French Romantic Movement, including Baudelaire, Gautier and Gérard de Nerval, and then returned in the Movement spearheaded by Huysmans, Lorrain and Remy de Gourmont, with Catulle Mendès providing a bridge between the generations, but in the medium of prose fiction, there was no stepping-stone sturdier than *La Bague d'Annibal* when it was written in 1834, and it was still remarkably innovative when it was belatedly published in 1842.

At the time of the novelette's first publication, many readers would have found Aloys not merely unsympathetic but incomprehensible, and the same might well be true today—which is where the whole merit of the story lies, and also any merit that the present translation might have. His is a story like no other, in more ways than one; readers cannot be required to sympathize with him, or even to comprehend him, any more than they can be required to sympathize with and comprehend his author, but they surely ought to find both of them intriguing, and challenging.

The issue of *Le Globe* in which *La Bague d'Annibal* first appeared is not reproduced on *gallica* and is presumably not preserved in the Bibliothèque Nationale, but Baudelaire's presentation copy of the Ducrey edition is reproduced on the website. Although the wording of that text seems to be identical to the version reprinted in the Alphonse Lemerre *Oeuvres de J. Barbey d'Aurevilly*, its layout differs. The Lemerre version, which appeared while Barbey was still alive (he died in 1889), presumably had the author's approval, but the alteration of the layout might not have been his idea.

The Lemerre version is odd because each of the 151 numbered "chapters" of the Duprey version commence on a new page, thus leaving a large amount of blank space in spinning out 16,000 words of text to 151 pages. The chapters correspond almost exactly (but not quite) to the paragraphing of the text. The narrative itself is fragmented, the intrusive narrator continually interrupting the story with digressions and comments, and the insertion of the additional page breaks emphasizes that fragmentation forcefully.

Because conventions of punctuation change over time, and differ between different languages, any translation is compelled to modify the punctuation of a text in rendering it from nineteenth-century French to twenty-first-century English. Whether that necessity gives a translator a right or a responsibility to alter the "big punctuation" of chapter breaks as well as the "small punctuation" of commas and dashes is perhaps a matter for debate, and perhaps the decision that I have made to remove the chapter numbers and page breaks from the present version of the story, while retaining the text-breaks, thus collapsing the layout of the text considerably, will probably seem to some readers to be audacious and impertinent. In making that decision, however, I have naturally asked myself: "What would

Barbey think?"—and I feel bound to assume that, even if he might not have approved entirely, at least he would have respected the decision and the spirit in which it was made.

This translation was mostly made from the version of the text contained in the volume of the *Oeuvres de J. Barbey d'Aurevilly* containing "L'Amour impossible" and *La Bague d'Annibal* published by Alphonse Lemerre; the specific edition I used was that of 1884. My failing eyesight, however, sometimes forced me to consult the version reproduced on wikisource.org—much easier to discern in mediocre light—which reproduces the same typesetting, but comes from a reprint with slightly different page numbers.

—Brian Stableford

HANNIBAL'S RING

The chariest maid is prodigal enough
If she unmasks her beauty to the moon.
Shakespeare[1]

WHY should I not tell you this story, Madame? You are doubtless too intelligent not to have moments of ennui like a stupid person, for the intelligent people of this interesting epoch have stolen the faculty of ennui from the stupid, who once had sole possession of it. So, if this story finds you in one of those terrible moments, so much the better for it, in truth. Even if it were worthless, it would be worth something if it interrupts your ennui. For myself, Madame, I have written it in the situation in which I would like you to be for reading it, which Byron doubtless recalled when he said, in his *Memoirs*, that writing *The Bride of Abydos* had prevented him from dying.[2]

---

1 *Hamlet*, Act 1 Scene 3, in the cautionary advice given by Laertes to his sister, Ophelia, while suggesting to her that it would be a bad idea to yield to Hamlet's entreaties.
2 Lord Byron published the "heroic poem" *The Bride of Abydos* in

This is also the story of a bride, but my poem is less ideal than his: the story of a bride, a pure bride, who became . . . but why say it? Continue reading, and you will know. I have spent my day by my fireside listening to the rain beating the windows, and this evening I remained without light for a long time watching the gleams of the fire dancing on the ceiling like specters, a very diverting thing for a person as melancholy as me. I could have gone out, going into society, but it would have required getting dressed, that great affair of life! And society, in spite of all its joys, is even sadder for me than solitude. I had only, therefore, the recourse of a cigar and tea, but the one gives me nausea and the other makes my head heavy and drowns my heart—the heart that it is always necessary, alas, to fish up again. It was not, therefore a resource. I would have been lost if I had not thought that a story to recount might carry me away.

And I have selected you for my audience, Madame, as Bossuet says, you and you alone, who would lend me your white ear if I asked you for that conduit; but I am not so demanding. I will not impose on you the necessity of listening to my story. Take it, leave it, forget

---

1814. He subsequently dismissed it as an item of hackwork, but that it not to say that writing it could not have "saved his life."

20

it or dream it. I am not speaking, I am writing, and you remain free. For myself, the changeability of women is sacred, and I no longer believe in anything but the divinity of caprice. Except that, if your eyes do not fall hereupon, you will never know that, one evening, when you were perhaps in society, ornamented, smiling and coquettish, for me, you had not quit your bedroom, and in curlers and a peignoir, your feet in the fireplace, on the same sofa, with the lamp behind us, you were listening to me. Are not the innocent pleasures of poetry worth as much to you as a reality?

In Paris, that winter, there was a young woman—but no one knew whether she was a maiden or a widow—who was the prettiest little phenomenon that it is possible to imagine, even with a great deal of imagination. As a name is forcibly necessary, I shall call her Madame d'Alcy—Joséphine d'Alcy. Joséphine is a name that throughout eternity, has been attached to those women of whom Madame d'Alcy was so completely, alas, the type-specimen. I know one of them, especially—but why speak ill?—who, if she read this story, might perhaps believe that I have wanted to trace a portrait. It is the mania of so many women to believe that one is always thinking about them!

Joséphine d'Alcy was twenty-seven years old, or so it seemed; for can one ever be sure of a woman's age? She was neither beautiful nor pretty, said the women who encountered her, but she did things "very well": a manner of agreeing that something is desolating and irresistible, a confession that seems disinterested. At any rate, that judgment was truer than a thousand others pronounced by those ladies, against which we, those of us hardened by indifference, never revolt, even though their impartiality appears to us to be a trifle suspect.

Joséphine, therefore, was neither beautiful nor pretty . . . but one sensed that, two days after having seen her, one could love her like a madman. She sank gently into the imagination, and then she remained there. She never produced the mysterious sympathy that is suddenly established between two hearts like an electric current, a subtle and hidden magnetism, the "thunderbolt" of the eighteenth century; no, she commenced by leaving one cold, or displeasing, but on seeing her a little more, she already displeased less, and finally, amour burst forth, all the stronger because of the time that it had taken to be born. I have always thought that individuals who are impressive in Joséphine's fashion are more dangerous than those who produce nervous intoxication at first sight.

She was blonde, the only color of youth; for, in spite of her birth certificate, no brunette woman was ever young. She was blonde. Lately, Madame, I have encountered a woman who is also blonde, like Joséphine, who would certainly have embarrassed the most skillful colorist if it were a matter of painting her. What he would have failed to do, I shall not attempt. Her hair had, as if sculpted by a superhuman procedure, and alive, the iridescence that spring sunlight caused to sparkle on newly-unfurled leaves. It resembled, in color, what the ever-undulating, never lost, curved line is in the marble of the Venus of the Medicis. Set against the oval of her cheek, her shoulders and her temples, in the roots of her blonde hair, there was, sometimes paling but eternally distinct, the gilded color in which the green leaves of the bouquet that she was holding in her amber hands were steeped . . . Of what substance was that woman? I don't know. She frightened me, although she was charming. In approaching her one would have respired her, perhaps faded . . . Her lover must have dreaded, every morning, having to put her in his herbarium.

Joséphine was not the strange, ungraspable blonde similar to the mysterious gold poured out by the emerald wing of a cantharides. The tawny reflection of her hair was extinguished beneath a pearl-gray nuance. There was nothing about her of springtime, vivacity, sparkle and freshness. Her forehead, which was slightly bulbous— the mask of a stubborn character—as well as her neck and shoulders, resembled slightly yellowed ivory. Her eyes were as blue and as stormy as the sea on the eve of a tempest, an indeterminate but somber color between olive and violet; one could not have seized her soul sideways. Her lip, of which the teeth broke the veins at every moment—a habitude of coquetry *à la Pompadour*, or perhaps repressed passion—was unhealthy and exhausted; but her smile expressed neither desire, nor tenderness, nor melancholy, that holy trinity of female smiles! When I looked at her, I could not help thinking of the Sphinx.

Many a time I had the temptation to palpate that long and gracious figure, to see whether some gryphon's wing was not hidden in the bosom, while my eye pursued at the hem of the floating dress the tip of a foot that made mock of the fable and said that the Sphinx was woman everywhere.

Oh, women, women, you are all more or less hypocritical. But people of the finest intelligence are sufficiently amiable not to have the slightest doubt in the presence of the Tartufferies of two beautiful dark eyes or the Machiavellianism of a pretty smile. Then, one reposes in error as in truth, and I even believe that repose in error is much more profound. Well, it was that security in deception, that frank illusion without afterthought that Joséphine never inspired. She did not deceive by means of a borrowed sentiment, but was the sentiment she expressed really her own? A question to embarrass the cleverest! She always produced doubt, she transpired anxiety. One did not know where one was with that strange creature, whose memories were hieroglyphs and the thoughts that appeared from time to time in her eyes were as problematic as sunspots and the blue lines that vein the yellow color of the moon.

Ah, by all the immortal gods, for us, the observers with square lorgnons and white gloves who surround the souls of women with the ring of their secret thought—an imperceptible ring that will often drive our marvelous skill to despair—Joséphine was a problem of transcendent imagination, the unknown to be deduced from a formidable equation. That supreme trickster, whom one takes at sixty for a man of genius, that composite of a whist-player and an old woman under the indolent appearance of a slumbering viper, Monsieur de Talleyrand himself, would have been easier to penetrate.[1]

For who was she, or what was she? Person or thing? Flesh or fish? Demon or angel? Or the Gordian knot of the demon and the angel, simply woman, that day-and-

---

1 The Duc de Talleyrand (1754-1838) became a legend in his lifetime by virtue of the skill that allowed his career as a diplomat and statesman to be transferred with ease from the service of Louis XVI to the Revolution, to Napoléon I, to the Bourbon Restoration and to Louis-Philippe.

night of the great masquerade of life? If I had been the great Newton himself, I would have given my theory of gravitation to know.

And, you see, I was not the only one to think like that. Joséphine excited an extreme curiosity. Her character, like her life, escaped everyone. Many people claimed to know her, but when they had said that the poor folk had said everything. What was her family? Where did she come from? Who the devil could boast of having encountered Monsieur d'Alcy? Like the Nile, she hid her origin in profound darkness, but that darkness did not have the effect on anyone of the night of time. It was an entirely modern rarity. It was said that she was shrewd rather than intelligent. However, her language was agreeable, especially when it commenced to dry up. She was a bluestocking of sorts, such as one sees nowadays, except that the blue of the stockings was celestial blue, a gently mitigated azure. It was only the garters of which one did not know the color.

She talked abundantly, in a vibrant voice; a blush sometimes rose to her cheeks and darkened there to scarlet, which cut abruptly through her mat complexion. She talked abundantly, for entire hours, gazing at her small hands, the wrists of which were so delicate that one trembled to see them detached with her bracelets when she took them off.

But what did she say? Charming trivia, cruel and common things, which society had taught her. She always gave a lesson of that catechism in drawing rooms that contained the entire secret of the morality of women; for one often has principles as one has a boudoir, in order to hide there. With the result that, except for the pleasure of an item of malicious gossip, the elegance of the phrasing—perhaps a little quintessential, it is true— and the aristocratic timbre of the voice, I would have liked her as much mute. In fact, a woman who talks is only a woman who talks, after all, but a mute woman is almost a statue, a statue without its disadvantages: the coldness of marble, the monotony of the pose and other inconveniences.

And besides, what does it matter what they say? When a talented larynx sings, who thinks of listening to anything but the larynx? Who thinks, for example, about the words of Monsieur Jouy, the illustrious author of *La Vestale*?[1] Women who, music apart, coo quite well, varying the role of a vestal virgin that they all play, more or less, in public, only pay attention to the sounds they are making. In what society teaches them, alas, is there

1 Étienne de Jouy supplied the libretto to Gaspare Spontini's opera *La Vestale* (1807).

anything better than sweet trivia in an operatic style? Except for you, Madame my reader, is there not always the same foundation of stupidity, with the sole difference of the voice?

And yet—why not confess it?—there was a kind of dissonance between Joséphine's voice and the words she repeated most frequently. Did she really think what she said? Eternal doubt, when it was a matter of that woman, fatal doubt that always recurred! And if she did not think it, why did she say it? But that is an abyss. Do women really know themselves the motives for their deceit?

But Joséphine did not deceive; once again, she embarrassed. If she had wanted to deceive she would easily have accomplished that facile thing. She would not have had that ironic and fugitive smile on her lips when she spoke about the duties of women and their destination down here, in a style—she had style at such moments— that would have done honor to Miss Edgeworth herself.[1] She would not have had that gaze, even more mocking than her smile, and that abandonment of the eyebrows even more mocking than her gaze!

---

1 The prolific Anglo-Irish novelist Maria Edgeworth (1768-1849), was very popular in France, although her refusal to avoid controversial political issues resulted in her being less favored in conservative England than her anodyne contemporary Jane Austen.

She had read Madame Necker de Saussure, and approved of her.[1] Many husbands swore to their wives that she would have been an excellent schoolteacher if hazard had placed her in a secondary condition, but the wives had their reasons for not agreeing entirely. And yet her morality was great, it seems, and her talents—as they say—were more numerous than was befitting for a woman of the world. One might have thought that she had been endowed by the fays, if the fays had no needs. She painted on ivory, she painted on enamel, she even painted on vellum when she gave her friends descriptions, in delectable handwriting, of her sentiments. She improvised on the piano as Corinne would have improvised if the piano had been in fashion in Corinne's time.[2] In sum, she succeeded in all the petty juggleries of a society as advanced as ours, with the superiority of an Indian or Chinese juggler, among her interesting compatriots.

---

1 Albertine Necker de Saussure (1766-1841), the daughter of a noted physicist and geologist, the sister of a famous chemist and plant physiologist, the wife of a noted botanist and the mother of a noted geologist, was a forceful advocate of education for women, a heroine to French *bas-bleus* in spite of being a Swiss Calvinist.
2 *Corinne* (1808) is a didactic novel by Madame de Staël, a great friend of Albertine Necker de Saussure, one of the great French *bas-bleus* and an important pioneer of the French Romantic Movement.

She pleased old women greatly, but young ones liked her a little less—something that could not seem strange, probably because the old women were not the only ones she pleased. They defended her in any encounter with the pleasant insinuations that slither even more guilefully than the advice of the serpent into Eve's ear, but, like the insinuations of those charming Eves that slip in their turn, into the ears of those good serpents, much less glibly. In fact, while awaiting Joséphine's first sin, they proclaimed her a coquette. A customary dilemma of those ladies! If one is sage, one is cruel and cold; if one takes pity, one is doomed.

Doomed? Yes!—dragged on the hurdle of all conversations, torn apart by all those hyenas of virtue who live on the dolors inflicted upon a poor amorous and imprudent woman, who lick her tears and find them tasty, and drink the blood from her heart in their carnivorous appetite for reputations. Did Joséphine fear those implacable women? Shakespeare has said, I don't know where, that the evil that is said of us is a culture, but did Joséphine understand hers as courageously? Was it cowardice that prevented her from being carried away, or the natural coldness of the pretty woman, a true glacier, whose husband said, throwing the key to her bedroom in the face of his friends: "Go and see!"? In any case, she could not be reproached for any false step, and yet, thousands of ferocious eagle eyes spied on her conduct from all directions; but not a single pearl had yet been detached from her necklace of good renown.

I don't know what she thought of men, but they always talked to her with amour or about amour, which is often the same thing. At least, I who am recounting this story, Madame, was like Mohammed's coffin drawn to the vault of the temple. I always came back to that topic of conversation. She contradicted my theories, and I thought—but was it an illusion?—that she only acted thus in order to exalt them further.

When I was at the height of my eloquence in my arguments, in which, in truth, there was enough to make a weak and naturally passionate woman die, like Semele in the presence of the divine lightning that consumed her, she was not moved at all; she had neither tears nor tender smiles, nor bewildered reveries, nor half-closed gazes, nor sudden blushes and faints. Only, my chagrined self-respect—vexed people pay themselves as they can—observed then that a kind of moist warmth, a transpiration of ardent desire, was exhaled from her prominent forehead under the unctuous pearl-gray hair. But that was only a mirage, which, like all mirages, only existed by virtue of the distance. For if, attracted by what I saw, I drew a little nearer to her, she was able to recoil her armchair with a splendor of prudery that would have made the reputation of an Englishwoman, and the mirage returned to the land of dreams, whence it had come.

Never did the most audacious of us feel her little hand tremble in his while dancing with her, or respond to eloquent pressures with one more tender and feebler. When she waltzed, perhaps she might have been more human; she did not have a strong enough head to resist the infernal spinning that causes dervishes to lose theirs . . . as well as so many women who do not spin, it is true, in that diabolical fashion purely and simply for the love of God. But like provincial virgins, Joséphine never waltzed.

Even more impatient than the most impatient, we looked that winter to the east and the west of all the drawing rooms to discover the man for whom we were waiting, as for a Messiah: the man whose predestined forehead would bear the mysterious star that would fascinate Joséphine. We were a sacred battalion of first-class observers, of those proud young men who still enjoy playing marbles after twenty-five but who will become, if God lends them life—or something else—moralists or Ministers of State; and, in spite of our prodigious sagacity, we did not see that radiant forehead appear over

which we would have raised the banners of vengeance
. . . unless, perhaps, it was—and why not?—the shiny
forehead crowned with silver hair of the honorable
Monsieur d'Artinel.

Monsieur d'Artinel—Baudouin d'Artinel, I believe . . .
yes, his name was Baudouin, or something very similar,
which one was always astonished to find attached to
such an individual—was a grave and respectable man,
enjoying public esteem to the highest degree, a counselor or judge of the royal court, I don't know which,
who had spent thirty years of his life, as everyone knew,
giving his wife three children and an unlimited number
of correspondents.

He had, therefore, been married, but his wife was dead.
He had wept, appropriately, for it was said that his marriage had once been a marriage of inclination. But time
kills dolor over the cadavers it makes, and in any case,
a counselor of the royal court cannot decently weep
forever. However, he had not put away his melancholy
air, and he still liked to slip in those words that resonate
so well in the ears of women when he wanted to make
allusion to ineradicable chagrins and cruel isolation.

Either because Joséphine had seduced him with the loquacity of her dresses and decorations or by her great speeches on virtue, public esteem or pure and tender sentiments, the venerable counselor sought the inexplicable creature avidly. Perhaps marriage and the difficulties that had followed it had not maltreated him enough for him not to perceive the external charms of Madame d'Alcy. His was a double and indecisive nature, half old fop and half sentimentalist, and it was thus that, tacking between those two ways of being, he had once passed for a man of good fortune.

Now, however, he was nothing more than a worn-out rake; he could weigh down his cravats and pad his garments, but he could not hide the insults of the years and the fatigues of the cabinet. He was not Caesar, but even Caesar had never been as bald. He had not lost his teeth, though, and on the whole, without looking too closely, he was a well-conserved man.

When Joséphine arrived somewhere, one could take it for granted that Monsieur Artinel would soon follow. People had commented on it at first, and then shut up, as he always arrived; habitude fatigues malevolent gossip, an inconstant person wants new sacrifices every day, like the divinities of Mexico who require a new human victim every morning.

He had stood up to that malevolent gossip better than one might have expected, for he was a man as submissive to public opinion as he was to etiquette: a magistrate who did not joke and who valued the consideration by which he had the good fortune to be surrounded, as he said himself, with a smile of proud forbearance. Perhaps he found that Joséphine was worth as much as that consideration, for which he had done everything— men forget in their old age—and felt disposed in favor of Joséphine to fly in the face of opinion, that queen of the world sacred by virtue of the cowardice of her slaves, whose humble and obedient servant he had been all his life.

And yet—I have already warned you, Madame. But I insist on the point further—Joséphine was not a superior woman, one of those women, daughters of our dreams, sirens who make us love the reef on which they will break us, irresistible creatures to whom one would sacrifice all the blood in one's heart and all the happiness of one's life. I often think, alas, that it would be a poor sacrifice.

No, she was a pretentious being, a simperer, who believed herself to be grace personified—a good reason for her not to be—an avalanche of big words, nonsense and stupidities, having to a supreme degree what all women have by right of birth and sex: an immense faculty to be false—although she was not—and above all, the prettiest slim and curvaceous figure. I could compare her to a wasp, if the comparison were not worn out: a wasp that had not ceased to be a woman, although she had conserved her sting.

Poor advantages, all that . . . except the maidenly figure, a svelte spindle on which, it seemed, Amour wound his sweetest dreams in vain. Poor advantages, all that; and yet all that would have been sufficient to knock over many philosophies and trouble the glorious monad of Leibniz himself . . . But Leibniz was very lascivious, I am told by my German master, very well-versed in biography; it is therefore necessary for us to choose another example—oh well!—to trouble that of Monsieur Baudouin d'Artinel, who was not a Leibniz, I assure you.

However, either because he had learned to master his penchants, because he had read in our modern works that profound sentiments render one serious, or because his habitude as a judge was more powerful than all the rest, if Monsieur Baudouin d'Artinel was in love with Joséphine—as some of us thought—he always conserved in society his sang-froid and his slightly plaintive gravity. Only, there was then a woman of intelligence, whom I knew, who always made that gravity dance a pretty little saraband on hot coals when she called him the model of husbands and fathers, and spoke to him about the fine qualities of his wife and the regrets that he conserved for her.

As for Joséphine, she was for Monsieur d'Artinel what she was for everyone. She could not be accused of simpering any more or less at him, although she had surely perceived that she interested the counselor to the highest degree. Do not all women, when they interest us, have a divine monitor which speaks to them about us in a whisper, a species of genius, like that of Socrates—but like that of Socrates not exactly counseling wisdom? Joséphine accepted without disturbance the discreet homages of Monsieur Baudouin d'Artinel. It is even believed that she might have been the best friend of his wife, if Madame d'Artinel had lived. At least, she and he, when they spoke about her, told one another that.

For they sometimes spoke about her. They spoke about her from the day when Monsieur d'Artinel had risked a eulogy to his wife, who, as she died, had taken all his affections with her—those affections which, since he had known Joséphine, no longer asked for anything but to return! That day, he had remarked, hopefully, a softening in Joséphine. Perhaps the tears that he thought he had seen in her eyes were the result of a stifled yawn, but whatever they might have been, she and he, from that day on, had shredded in their melancholy conversations an infinite quantity of scabious petals. It is sometimes an excellent means of making oneself loved to regret a dead wife, and who knows whether Monsieur d'Artinel, with his experience of the nature of women, had not thought that his might be of precious utility with regard to Joséphine?

One evening, at the home of Madame Doril, Joséphine was chatting, as usual, while looking at her pretty rose-colored claws, which the brush and the lemon had smoothed with so much care. There were a lot of people in the drawing room. She was sitting next to the curtain of the window, a curtain of blue silk in the undulations of which she was drowning her ash-blonde hair. Her lips were moving like the strings of a harp when pinched by a rapid hand.

But no one heard what she was saying. For the first time, she was no longer speaking in a high-pitched and metallic voice, either because her voice was lost in the noise of the conversations that were going on around her, or because she wanted to hide from everyone else what she was only saying to one person alone.

For she was speaking to one alone—one alone, who was gazing at her, leaning on the arm of his chair, as Napoléon must have done when looking at a map of Russia before his unfortunate campaign. Still speaking, she was only posing on the surface of the gaze of the man who was listening to her the vague and mobile radiance of her own: one of those gazes that brush and skim but never settle. At the summit of the triangle of which those two persons formed the base, in the corner of the drawing room, stood Monsieur d'Artinel.

"Can you tell me," he asked me, with an expression more ridiculous than it is permissible for a counselor to have—and yet God knows with what munificence that permission has been accorded to all the jurisconsultants on earth!—"who the Monsieur is to whom Madame d'Alcy is speaking at the moment, at the other extremity of the room?"

I looked. "That Monsieur, as you put it, Monsieur," I replied, "is named Aloys de Synarose. All that I know about him is reduced to a few small details: he has intelligence, although that intelligence is slightly spoiled by affectation, the manners of a fop, and, it is said, a great obstinacy."

And I bowed to Monsieur d'Arsinel who repeated: "A great obstinacy!" without returning my salute.

Oho! I said to myself. *Is Monsieur Artinel, Monsieur Baudouin d'Artinel, jealous?* And I looked at the Othello of the royal court, with his white cravat, which did not have a crease, and his black coat, of the finest luster. *Is it really you who is attained by that picturesque passion?*

※

Yes, he was jealous. He was jealous: atrocious torture! He was jealous on the basis of less than a word, a sign or an air! He was jealous on the basis of something trivial, as one is jealous, even if one is a judge, as he was, and he would still have been jealous if he had been an entire court of justice on his own! A terrible presentiment had passed under his irreproachable quilted waistcoat like a whirlwind. He had suddenly gone pale; his nose had twitched in a formidable fashion, as if he had the Quinola in a game of reversis.[1] He was jealous, for sure! In spite of the habitual dignity of his pose, he did not impose as much as Ali de Janina when his moustache bristled with fury, but it is certain that the few gray hairs that designed a pale and ideal crown on his occiput would have stood on end at the sight of Aloys if they had not been thoroughly steeped that day in oil of Macassar.[2]

It was the judgment of society on Aloys that I had given to Monsieur Baudouin d'Artinel. Why would I have said any more to him? Did not Monsieur d'Artinel have the ideas of society? Did he not hold to the consideration that society dispenses? Was he not a child of society who had become one of its doctors? Was he not one of the elements, the number of which, in order to make a public, had embarrassed Beaumarchais? Through the epidermis, did he see the man? And the man is almost always flayed!

1 Reversis was a trick-taking card game ancestral to the modern Hearts and Black Maria, which gradually evolved a bizarre complexity, in which the jack of hearts, known as the Quinola after a Spanish admiral, played a key role.
2 Ali Pacha de Janina was the governor of Epirus in the Ottoman Empire at the end of the nineteenth century. A colorful account that he gave of his exploits to a French consul was appropriated by Alexandre Dumas for recycling in the second collection of his *Les Crimes celebres* (1840), and he made a brief but crucial appearance in *Le Comte de Monte Cristo* (1844), which naturally made him a legendary figure in France.

But society is an old blind man who pretends to be able to see, and who perennially mistakes black for white with an imperturbable sang-froid. Society is Brid'oison personified—he was also a counselor, like Monsieur Baudouin d'Artinel—applying the rules of a murderous jurisprudence rightly or wrongly.[1] Society is imbecility multiplied by itself and elevated to its highest power. For it is only idiots who sense nothing weakening in their entrails when they cut throats—and society cuts throats so frequently!

That is society! Oh, keep well away from it, all of you who have a heart to lacerate and a pride that can be made to suffer. You, Madame, who are reading these lines, perhaps you love it dearly and do not know it! Alas, I knew it well at an early hour. There is not one poor daisy of my youth on which it has not drooled its venom. There is not one of my joys that has not been poisoned at the source. It has attached itself to people I loved because I loved them; it has struck them because I loved them; it has made me witness the spectacle, bound and gagged and devoid of vengeance.

Yes, bound by the conventions of that society, by the laws of that heartless society; obliged to feign a serene

---

1 Brid'oison is the rigidly uncompromising judge in Beaumarchais' *Le Mariage de Figaro* (1778).

countenance, biting my heart on my lips and swallowing it in my breast when it was about to escape; drinking my tears internally, a bitter beverage! For I had not, like Achilles, distant shores, a tent on some strand, the vast bosom of the ocean or a friend, my mother Thetis or Patroclus, to hide them.

But pride was the column against which I set my back, the stake to which they had tied me, which prevented me from buckling. Like Jesus in the bloody flagellation, I did not fall under their blows, and like him, I did not send them any words begging for mercy. And you, the Saint Sebastians of this world, the martyrs of your amour for me, I pressed your torn breast to my torn breast more preciously and even more tightly, as if the arrows that had pierced you had been able to come away and return to my heart alone.

Society, therefore, said of Aloys that he was a fop—one of those beings as dry as the skin of which their gloves are made—a kind of Lauzun who would have his boots removed by the hands of a princess if those hands had still been there![1] Only, fop as he might have been, society

---

1 Armand Louis de Gontaut, Duc de Lauzun, later Duc de Biron (1747-1793) fought in the American Revolution before becoming a commander in the French Revolutionary Army, but was guillotined during the Terror for excessive leniency toward opponents

tolerated his conceit because it was accompanied by the most frightening facility in adapting epigrams. In matters of ridicule, Aloys loaded his rifle with large-caliber bullets. In consequence, there was a frightful mess when he let rip. "What an amusing scourge!" said the most courageous women, whom his conversation interested so much that they were only afraid of him by reflection. Was it for that, or because Rivarol wore a pink jacket, that they had nicknamed him Rivarol II?[1]

But I have read somewhere the Rivarol was handsome, and that that was half of his prodigious wit—for women. Aloys was not so magnificently endowed. He was ugly, or at least he believed himself to be; it had been repeated to him so frequently during his childhood, when the heart blossoms and one loves with the energy and freshness, a profound but rapid vitality, of creatures at their dawn.

Even Aloys' mother, his tender mother—which is to say, the person who sees nothing of the faults of her children through the sublime illusion of her tenderness—had

---

of the regime. The princess to whom the text refers was Amélie de Boufflers, Princesse de Luxembourg, to whom he was married against his will by his family, and whom he did not treat well.

1 The reference is to the reactionary royalist writer Antoine de Rivarol (1753-1801), famous for his epigrams.

mocked his ugliness as an unkind stepmother might have done, when she found his kisses less welcome because they did not resemble the desired image of which she had dreamed for a long time: an immaterial amour, that maternal amour! Was it not Chateaubriand who concluded the immortality of the soul therefrom, as if, in every case, the entire human race had worn skirts?

Now, those first impressions are so obstinate, they plunge in certain natures to such great depths, that they remain there forever, like bullets that the surgeon's knife cannot extract, and over which the flesh has closed up: a comparison all the more exact because the impressions, like the bullets, cause all our blood to retreat on certain days.

And those memories of his childhood were so vivid in Aloys that perhaps twenty women who had avenged him for the distaste of a father and a mother—models of amiable solicitude who could not bear the idea that their son was not a handsome boy—had not effaced the trace of the bitter mockery, a corrosion that did not burn his cheek, but his thought . . . when he thought of it.

A great soul, however, that Aloys—but the Ocean, which engulfs cliffs, also rolls aquamarine in its bosom; he had had space enough within him for all the dolors that met in his soul to live there without friction. That immeasurable and solitary grandeur, the moral strength that had once rendered the squashed nose of Socrates superb, often cast august reflections over Aloys' pale temples, and women, at those superb hours, remained paler than him and confounded, as if Heaven had been suddenly revealed, although it was only the man's mask that had been opened.

For he had a mask: a mask of iron padlocked behind his head, the key to which he had thrown in the sea; a mask harder and colder than that of the adulterous brother of Louis XIV,[1] for it was scorn that had forged it and pride that had sealed it there. He did not want men to rejoice in having wounded him, if they could still wound him. He did not want a noble and grave idea

---

1 The prisoner held incommunicado in various French jail between 1670 and 1703 who became known as "the man in the iron mask" (although the mask he was forced to wear was only black cloth) obtained an extra dimension of posthumous notoriety when Voltaire's one-time secretary, the self-styled Chevalier de Mouhy, wrote a sensational novel proposing that he had been imprisoned because he was Louis XIV's illegitimate older brother and thus a plausible heir to the throne. The hypothesis was repeated by Voltaire in the *Encyclopédie* and modified by Alexandre Dumas, who featured the case in *Les Crimes célèbres* and subsequently made him Louis XIV's identical twin in his sequel to *Les Trois mousquetaires*, *Le Vicomte de Bragelonne, ou Dix ans plus tard* (1847-50).

to be welcomed by laughter or indifference. He had the modesty of thought and an even more chaste pride of sentiment.

He had all that, but he kept it between himself and God, the discreet confidant of all futile superiorities. If he had known women less, one could have believed that he was keeping those pearls of the soul for his adored future, which do not dispense with the other jewel-case; but he was too well aware that one coifs oneself with a cameo, and that moral things do not look well in the hair, to act in that manner. The best of him thus remained within him, and above it he had put what is worth more than the four claws of a lion crossed over our heart in order to defend it: the pleasantry that has wings, and which jealous pedants, in their leaden style, call frivolity. Like the famous garment that Jean Bart wore for an entire day,[1] the splendid silver breeches lined with cloth of gold, which had the cruel effects of a cilice, the inverse was even more precious than the place of his person; and, as Jean Bart was a victim of his lining, it was also the most beautiful and the most intimate part of his soul that caused him the most pain.

---

1 Jean Bart (1650-1702) was a French privateer, who distinguished himself so spectacularly fighting for France against the Dutch that he was eventually promoted to the rank of admiral in the navy. A fanciful biography of him by Edward Mangin published in 1828 relates how, when he was first summoned to Louis XIV's court, he commissioned a tailor to make him a coat, waistcoat and breeches of gold brocade lined with silver tissue, but the latter irritated him horribly and made him a laughing-stock.

In all the cups of life into which he had plunged his lips he had drunk a bitter absinthe that he always rediscovered on his lips. An eternal irony dictated his words, an irony so profound that nothing in the softness of his voice and the courtesy of his language, betrayed its secret. Others, however, sensed an insulting power that toyed with them through the gracious words. They sensed that just as, on hearing a harmonica—celestial music, indescribable pleasure!—one feels that one is about to faint.[1]

That evening, however, he spoke less to Joséphine than he listened to the ravishing doll—except that, from time to time, his lips were seen to move, which allowed a remark to fall: a simple remark, which she picked up, and around which she wound her thought for a quarter of an hour, if one can call the frail product of Madame d'Alcy's gaseous brain by that ambitious word. They were talking—or, to put it more accurately, she was talking—about animal magnetism.

---

1 The reference is not to the instrument nowadays known as a harmonica, or mouth-organ, but to a previous French instrument which had that name until the new invention usurped it in the 1830s. It consisted of an arrangement of steel bars made to vibrate with a bow.

The result of that evening was the disappointment of the good Monsieur d'Artinel, who shuffled his feet while talking politics with a fat general who had pinned him by the fireplace. From that fireplace he directed an anguished gaze from time to time at Joséphine and her fortunate partner . . . at Joséphine, who would not—at least, it seemed so to him at the distance where he was placed—have picked up a world if she had had it at her feet. That was also the opinion of Aloys when he stood up from Joséphine's chaste flanks, and we had asked him what he thought of her.

"My God," he said nonchalantly "she's a stupid woman who has just enough jargon to impose on people more stupid than her"—a judgment more cynical, in truth, than we had expected on his part. "She isn't pretty," he continued, "and you can see her from here rolling her head with so much affectation in that curtain of blue, less pale than she's pale blonde. Word of honor, her complexion is blonder than her hair. I believe that, if she had a lover, she would fake tears very artistically on the paper of the letters that she wrote to him, with a few drops from the glass of orange-flower water that she drinks before going to bed."

Having said that, Aloys no longer occupied himself with Joséphine, and he was wittier than ever with us. The next day he saw her again at the home of Madame de Dorff, where both of them often went. After a month of almost daily encounters, I asked Aloys one evening whether he still had the same opinion of Joséphine. "Yes, still," he replied, with a sang-froid all the more admirable because he was madly in love with her.

Are you, by chance, astonished, Madame, by what happened to Aloys? Is it the first time that a fact as insolent in its truth as a street-porter has come along to knock down the slightly foolish theory of the ideal love of the German mystical imagination? For myself, having a certain inclination toward exalted mysticism, albeit in a different manner from Doctor Kant, and an understanding of reality to a very superior degree, the woman that I have loved most—and I certainly loved her a great deal—was the opposite of everything that I would have wanted.

He loved her madly—yes, in him amour had the intensity of madness, but there the analogy stops dead. Reason remained to him, strong, inflexible and inalterable, and although he loved that woman, he applied a set-square to her in his thought and leveled her with a judgment that never softened.

For he was of that savage and slightly proud race of men for whom nothing in life is illusion, possessed of piercing eyes that see the wrinkle beside the beloved mouth and the poverty of the heart that they press against their own heart most amorously: eagles who, if they couple, rip apart the female in their caresses, as being unworthy of their imperial nests, and, if they become fathers, break in their claws one morning the fragile egg or the birds without talons, too feeble to resist them, as they once bruised the breast of their decrepit father with a nonchalant thrust of their great wing.

Men who have no respect for anything on earth, whom society accuses of egotism because their self is greater than society, and of malevolence because their implacable eye has seen all hidden motives: for men of that sort, Petrarchan amour is impossible. If they sometimes say many sornettes,[1] they make very few insolent sonnets! For them, a woman, that angel of dubious purity, is only a more or less pretty succubus. When they come to your home, Madame, have the porter tell them that you are not in.

---

1 I have left this term untranslated in order to preserve the wordplay; it means "silly things."

But no—rather receive them, Madame; make their eyes soften and you will be avenged; for those men have a heart that you can tear into a thousand pieces, like the frailest of your fabrics, and pierce with laughter like one of your festoons with your steel punch. Only—annoying, is it not, Madame?—although one can desolate them, they will console themselves; they will not die of it. It is with their wit that they bandage their wounds: an immortal balm that always saves them. More fortunate than Mohammed, there is no Fatima who can poison them, or, if there is, the poison is futile: they are the Mithridates of amour. It is not them who have invented the touching but commonplace symbol of the ivy that dies where it attaches itself. More often than the most flexible creepers, they can detach themselves very easily without dying of it.

And why should they not detach themselves, Madame? They have received too generous a share from Heaven not to make use of the dangling grace of clematis; and besides which—I beg your pardon if you are European, and above all French—on many points, although sensitive, they approach the opinions of that false and abominable Prophet who only had ideas regarding women worthy of a camel-driver. In their eyes, as in his—alas,

I blush to say it, a woman being for me a Madonna, a beautiful white form (when she is white, that is) to invoke at the foot of an altar—in their eyes, woman is, after all, only a cushion on a more or less perfumed divan, a delightful divan-cushion for sleeping, yawning and . . . making love!

And yet, in spite of his impertinent opinions, a man is consecrated to such inconsequence that he would overturn the world for a mere divan cushion! How many times he has been seen—perhaps by you, Madame?—unhappy, and unhappy to the point of delirium, because cushion A, for example, is not in the place of cushion B. That is what happened one day to Aloys de Synarose, as it had already happened to Monsieur Baudouin d'Artinel.

It is necessary that I put a story within this story. One of my best friends, Madame, claimed, with the customary conceit of smitten hearts, to have for a mistress the most ravishing creature in the world, from head to heels, inclusively. I have twenty friends who have a very similar pretention on their own account, and who even believe what they say . . . which is too much. But the man of whom I speak was firmer in his belief than all the others when he spoke about his good fortune. If I had been able to paint under his dictation as I can write here, we would have one portrait more and we would be able to judge whether the ensemble responded to the details. A portrait is a precious relic for a man in love! But bah! Every portrait is a lie or an impotence, and as a memory, I prefer of my mistress what the practical joker Bonaparte bequeathed to his mother in his testament.[1]

Yes, painters lie in the throat, the hand, the color and the thought when they imagine retracing adored features for us, and which we have the cowardice to suffer! If they were Raphael himself—the chaste Raphael who died in the noxious bed of a courtesan but whose thought never placed the tip of its white angelic foot where he was not ashamed to place his drunken lips—they would not be worthy to retrace one whose image has passed indelibly into our hearts at a glance, one single glance: the veil of Saint Veronica, but on which the blood that paints the adored head is ours, not hers.

Without a doubt, the friend that I am citing to you Madame, thought thus about the annihilation of those jewels that amour sometimes exchanges, and over the absence of which it weeps when it does not have the sad courage to break them. The sacred image reposed within his breast, and not above it, at the end of a worn ribbon.

---

1 A hank of his hair made into a bracelet with a small gold clasp.

Except, by virtue of I know not what further tender inconsequence, he had painted himself one feature—just
one—of his mistress, and at least there was in that idea
an entire divine mystery of the soul, which enabled the
exigency of his abused senses to be pardoned.

It was an eye—right or left I cannot say—but it was
a pale blue eye like a Parma violet, as luminous as the
dew; as sparkling and melancholy as a star but, like that
of Hesperus, in a sky in which it is still alone! A gentle
and benevolent star that allowed itself to gaze in the
aureole of its golden ashes without punishing you for
it with a tear, an April sunlight that seemed to emerge
from a tempestuous horizon; for the contour of that eye,
so fresh and so pure, was plunged in a somber night.

And I understand that fantasy! Did not Pascal, that lynx
of Jansenism, who bloodied all human thought with the
bristles of his cilice, ask somewhere whether it is the
nose or the ears that we love in the beloved woman? To
love the eye of one's mistress is to love thought itself:
thought blossoming in a charming flower illuminated
by a divine daylight; thought that languishes or smiles
but always attracts . . . and sometimes also rejects us.

Days of migraine—or, even worse, caprices. But were they Joséphine's eyes that Aloys would have had painted on his chocolate box, or her bulbous forehead, or her lip incessantly bitten by a teasing tooth, or something even more voluptuous? The other day, Madame, I was thunderstruck by the diamond-shaped pleat of a satin dress.

I do not know what that accursed robe covered. If I had been able to know I would not have wanted to know, but that pleat was crumpled by the devil himself! That dress was the tender and serious cloth that we call *manteau de La Vallière*,[1] and either because of the superstition of that name, so gentle and melancholy in its charm, or because of a more ardent impression, I stopped before the woman wearing the Carmelite colors with such an attractive softness and I saw what I ought not to recall.

Let us rather get back to our story, Madame. If it were you, I would still dream about you, but you have forgotten me; it is better, therefore, to return to Aloys. Aloys

---

1 Louise de La Vallière (1644-1710) was Louis XIV's mistress from 1661 to 1667. I can find no evidence for the cited phrase being commonly applied to a fabric, although an upholstery fabric named after her, a kind of necktie and a kind of damask still survive, fugitively, so the reference might be to the last-named.

had sworn to himself never to talk about his amour to Joséphine, and he had sufficient mastery of his nerves to keep the word he had given himself as if he had given it to someone else. I am convinced that you scarcely care for Aloys, Madame. One never knows where one is with such men, and women, those naïve persons, love immensely abandoning them to others.

At least, my hero said to himself, *I won't be deceived by her. She'll no longer play with my heart, the gracious she-cat, as if with a ball of thread. And if, one day, she deceives someone else, she won't display my letters, my hair or the sadness of my brow like a trophy of weapons. I want to break her vanity like glass under my pride.*

I want to break . . . ! And he was broken himself by the stoical resolution he had made; but, inimitable in his fractures, he was not downcast. Like Diogenes, who rolled in the ardent sand under the most devouring summer sun, he exposed himself without flinching to all the bitterness of a compressed passion. He gazed at himself impassively, burning his heart, as Scaevola watched his hand burn.[1] To suffer, for him, was to live; it was to

---

1 Gaius Mucius, nicknamed Scaevola [left-handed], was a legendary Roman youth allegedly sent to assassinate Lars Porsena during the siege of 508 B.C. He failed and was captured; he supposedly put his right hand in a fire as an act of defiance and was released.

fulfill his human vocation; if he had had post-horses
with which to flee his dolor, he would have refused to
mount them.

Everywhere that he encountered Joséphine—and he
encountered her everywhere—he showed her the coquetry of wit that he had with all women. He believed
that he had penetrated her—a bitter science, a glance
for which one pays dear—but he remained impenetrable. He addressed the same flatteries to her, with
a voice as light, as to the most indifferent women. It
would have been impossible to perceive through his
manners that the woman in question was anything else
to him than, at the most, a pretty thing. I observed that
he was always a little paler in her presence . . . but the
difference was slight.

Pallor over pallor: the sign of passionate natures when
they are suffering or enjoying themselves; for then the
blood retreats to the heart like a river flowing back to its
source. Alas, Joséphine did not have the secret of that
pallor, scattered flakes fallen that morning on yesterday's
slightly-hardened snow, which the slightest breeze car-
ries away!

She loved—who can say why?—to converse for hours with Aloys, and yet she always emerged from those interminable conversations discontented with herself and him. Certainly, he had not said a word that was inappropriate. Louis XIV, that king of propriety, was no more so than Aloys. Oh, my God, perhaps it was for exactly that reason that she was discontented! If he had been carried away momentarily, if a thought that was too narrow had punctured his speech, that might have been allowed to pass as an impertinence; she was clever, she was supple, she had fingernails, she was a woman, she would have had an advantage; but it was necessary to submit entirely to Aloys' superiority.

Was that not very harsh, Madame? Aloys had the serenity of a sage. A sage is very irritating! He had the serenity of a sage, but a sage at whom one does not laugh, for beneath that sagacity there was power. That was not visible, but it was tangible. So, after one of those irreproachable conversations, Joséphine went home fatigued, exhausted and annihilated, with warm sweat on her brow and her nerves jangling—for Aloys had, as always, led her to say much more than she wished. In vain, she promised herself that she would stiffen herself at the earliest opportunity; Aloys' conversation resembled a roller-coaster; once departed, one could not stop.

Does he love me? she asked herself, smiling like a spoiled child at her mirror. The mirror said yes, but vanity still doubted. For the first time in her life, vanity, that flattering mirror, seemed to her to reflect less beautifully than the one in her boudoir. She trembled as she gazed into it

I shall soon know, she went on. Charming dreamer! Her elbow leaning on the marble of the mantelpiece, one might have thought her a poor amorous young woman. *Be careful, Fanny, you're going to break the laces of my corset!*

※

I shall know tomorrow! But the eternal tomorrow never came. The entire winter passed thus. There was not a single one of those magnificent and imperceptible feminine ruses employed since Eve all the way to the Marquise du V***[1] of which she did not make use in order to discover whether Aloys loved her, but alas, it was

---

1 This reference is unclear. A notorious eccentric named the Marquis du Vivier flourished in 1834, and there is now a kind of champagne wine known as Marquise du Vivier, but that is probably a coincidence. The *du* is probably a misprint and the person the author might well have had in mind the Marquise de Vichet, who was one of Chateaubriand's most passionate correspondents; her name was rendered in his published correspondence as the Marquise de V***. His side of the correspondence maintained his typical attitude of cool and studied ennui, which might well have served as a model for Barbey and Aloys.

futile. She even went as far as coquetries—but virtuous coquetries—with Monsieur Baudouin d'Artinel.

As for her, perhaps she experienced the sole species of sentiment to which she was susceptible: a sharp, burning, incessantly stimulated curiosity; and doubtless, in conversations so long and so replete with the metaphysics of the heart, in the intoxication of flowers, candles, music and dancing, she found at those moments the singular sensation of which Ninon de Lenclos spoke, and of which men are so unfortunate as to be unaware.

A vivid emotion without a name came and soon passed, similar to the light and dewy foam of a bottle of sweet Burgundy kept on ice. She had not been kneaded by a burning dust, and I have more lava in my pipe than entered into the composition of her entire person.

One day—it was in the month of May, the seventeenth of May (I love dates in love stories: they resemble little ivory sticks on which memories, those bullfinches with bloody breasts, can perch more conveniently)—Aloys had spent the entire day in the country. The body, in that elegant Stoic, was less robust than the soul. By dint of suffering mentally he was gripped by a stomach-ache, a commencement of a cough and an inflammation of the brain, still slight, it is true, but which might aggravate—a pleasant hope! His physician had employed gum,[1] leeches and asses' milk.

He went to spend a few days, as the first roses bloomed, at the château of Madame de Dorff, Josephine's great friend, one of those good friends, of whom it is so nice and consoling to have when one is a woman—for it is rare to have two; one of those liaisons that console her and avenge her for the perfidies of men, although evil tongues claim that two women cannot love one another.

And that damned opinion I once held, Madame. I had remarked the gaze that two women dart at one another when they meet for the first time, whether in a drawing room, at the theater or even in church . . . and frankly, that diabolical glance confirmed me in my detestable belief; but that excessively precipitate judgment gave way to a saner and more accurate appreciation of things when I saw a woman sacrifice her lover heroically to

---

1 Given the reference to Aloys' cough, the *gomme* in question would probably have been *gomme adragan*, known in English as gum tragacanth, a popular herbal remedy of the day.

her friend—it is true that she took another—and a governess who wanted to enable her pupil, whom she no longer wanted, to marry.

O amity, amity! Sentiment of the ages between themselves, attempted by humans down here—it's true that I prefer a quilted dressing-gown for the winter—O amity, you are nothing less than the most spiritual impulse of the heart, the most noble aspiration of thought! I no longer know which sculptor, in order to express the divine essence, represented two beautiful naked children, a boy and a girl, kissing one another in a saintly fashion on the mouth: a bold idea that J. J. Rousseau—the most banal of lackeys—dared to call an obscenity. Oh, it was two young women that it was necessary to sculpt thus in order to express you, O amity! But perhaps someone would find that to be a nonsense even more than another obscenity.

Madame de Dorff was, therefore, Joséphine's friend—a very rare friend, as my grandmother said in departing from the thousandth that she had had. Madame de Dorff was no longer young; she put on rouge like Jezebel. Joséphine was therefore able to love her. If we had been in the eighteenth century, Joséphine, the enigmatic Joséphine, whose ribbons were always fresh and came from we knew not where, would perhaps have been Madame de Dorff's Mademoiselle Aïssé,[1] whereas she was only her "dear beauty," an official title of no great value. Madame de Dorff adopted with her the maternal airs of a patroness so dear to women on the wrong side of forty. If she had known about Aloys' passion for Joséphine she would doubtless have said to him: "Thank you for loving her"—a historic phrase that I heard uttered by one of those friends, who repeated: "Poor child, how she compromises herself!" to a man who was dying of a sublime passion.

Now, Aloys returned to Paris. As he was about to depart, Madame de Dorff said, with that aristocratic assurance that does not fear a refusal, the aplomb of a well-born woman who imposes a desire like a law even on an indifferent individual: "Monsieur de Synarose, if I dared I would ask you to give this smelling-salt bottle to Madame d'Alcy. I was suffering so much in my farewell visit that I took it with me. Will you thank her for me and tell her that I am quite well now?"

---

1 Charlotte Aïssé (c1694-1733) became celebrated posthumously when Voltaire edited and published the letters she wrote to her friend Madame Calandrini. She had had a colorful past, having become the mistress of the Regent, Philippe d'Orléans, after being brought to Paris as a child by the French ambassador to Constantinople, who had bought her there following her capture in Circassia.

It was the first opportunity that had presented itself for
Aloys to see Madame d'Alcy at her home. She did not
receive men there. A mysterious retreat in which no
booted foot ever penetrated, her boudoir only opened
to women, for she was too young and in too delicate a
position, since she had no husband and could not claim
any relative, to see anyone at home but a few young
women and many of those respectable dowagers who
shield a reputation so well against the thrusts of malevolent gossip, and who still occupy themselves with the
pleasures of young men—but in an orthodox fashion—
by enabling them to make good marriages.

Aloys took the bottle from the hands of Madame de
Dorff: a charming agate bottle as obscure as a woman's
thought, but which exhaled beneath its sculpted golden
stopper a vague odor of essence of vervain, the magical
and sacred plant with which witches once crowned their
foreheads—the witches of today only carry it in their
little bottles. Aloys promised that he would return the
bottle to Madame d'Alcy that same evening.

He went there. She was alone. He would have preferred
to see her flanked by a few of those experienced virtues
by whom she was usually surrounded, but she was alone,

65

and the first ten minutes of a tête-à-tête with the woman one loves are not the moment to show vulgar embarrassment. He did not want to lose the equilibrium of his conceit, even on Madame d'Alcy's carpet or sofa.

She was sitting languidly on a kind of low divan, an item of Oriental furniture that reminded her of the existence of odalisques in the bosom of her chaste solitude. She was sitting languidly—idle and probably bored by having been alone for such a long time. Was she waiting? The devil alone might know. Her dress—for the dress is part of the personality of a woman, and I am never able to separate them—was an indecisive color, a slightly hermaphrodite hue between gray and lilac. One might have thought it a capricious cloud woven for her, one of those vapors of a spring evening behind which one imagines the most delightful horizons.

But I have never been able to describe, and I will skip over, such details. She was, therefore, idle and languid. Why was she languid? She did not know, but it was a pose, and Lady Hamilton[1] herself did not have more

---

1 Emma, Lady Hamilton (1768-1815) was immortalized by the painter George Romney, who produced multiple portraits of her in various costumes and poses while she was known as Emma Hart (her real name was Amy Lyon), prior to her marriage and during her subsequent attainment of the height of her celebrity as Lord Nelson's mistress.

artistry in posing than Joséphine—it is true that her studies of the antique had been less profound; and as for those of the nude, no one can say anything about them, but it is impossible to have a more pensive attitude. I adore those inclined foreheads in which the shadow always floats of something: a reverie that is passing, returning or remaining, like the image of a willow weeping over the water. That evening, she had an expression even more pensive than usual. I can well believe it; she was a woman who was always thinking . . . about having the air of thinking.

With a firm hand, Aloys, his breast shaken by the palpitations of his heart on finding himself alone with that woman, handed Joséphine the bottle with which Madame de Dorff had charged him. Then a conversation commenced, which, at the third phrase, as perpetually happened between them, suddenly turned to the mysteries or mysticisms of sentiment.

Those conversations are more dangerous than walking on the tips of steeples. They have made more Françoises de Rimini[1] than the tenderest books in the world, read

---

1 Françoise de Rimini is the French rendering of the name of Francesca da Rimini (c1255-c1285), immortalized by Dante in the *Inferno* with her adulterous lover Paolo Malatesta, the couple being eternally trapped by a symbolic whirlwind.

in tête-à-tête with a handsome young man. It is the Poul-Sherro[1] of many innocences. Aloys was admirable in his empire over himself, for he sensed that he had never been more loved. Oh, if he had been able to touch Joséphine with a magic wand and put her to sleep on her divan, what kisses he would have distributed over that gently curved forehead, over the vellum of that mat complexion and in her parted lips—the calyx of a rose, slightly yellowed but still so sweet! But Aloys' magic wand was a marvelous wit, which did the opposite of putting the people it touched to sleep.

His pride certainly whispered to him that if he cared to dare, the audacity might perhaps succeed. He had the high opinion of it that a man who wants a woman always has—an opinion that, to tell the truth, approaches insolence, and which women scarcely pardon, apparently because such impertinence puts them in the necessity of resisting.

But he did not *want* her, because he was scornful of her. And yet he was thirsty, and the lake was flowing at the edge of his lips. He experienced the desire of the

---

1 The author presumably found Poul-Sherro in *Philosophie de la religion* (1838) by P. Véry , where it is allegedly the bridge to Paradise in the mythology of the Turks, although it is hard to find other sources confirming the allegation.

rapacious hands that will enable us clasp to our breasts of flesh, it seems, the stars of the most distant stars. Oh well! He had put that desire in the handcuffs of his will . . . Joséphine did not suspect his torments for a moment. At any rate, who can say whether Aloys' Spartan strength might not have succumbed if the tête-à-tête had lasted any longer? When he got up, he was more fatigued than Madame de Staël after a winter of conversations.

Certainly, he was not at the bottom of the staircase when Joséphine pushed away with chagrin the white velvet stool on which she had displayed her foot at all angles while Aloys was still there. A difficult thing to digest! She was conscious of the skill and the futility of her gestures; Aloys continued to escape all the ambushes, so well set, and so perfectly planned! The disappointment was so great and so profoundly felt that, after reflection, she thought about risking a letter: the primary imprudence of passion, the "abyss that invokes all the others," as the Bible says.

For it is better to give one's person than to write, and by Jupiter, Madame, that is not a paradox, like those I sometimes sustain. I love paradox, it is true; my birth was one itself, my mother having introduced me into the world on the day when one celebrates all those who have departed from it: a festival of heirs, in which we seem to say to the poor dead: "Wherever you are, accept our sentiments, and stay there!"[1]

But this is not a paradox; it is a trivial, vulgar, worn-out truth—if the truth were not as eternal as those to whom we owe yearly rents—and within the range of all. A letter is an eminently compromising thing, a species of official statement that establishes as certain a fact that it would be better to forget. At least, when one has put up the loosened curls of one's hair again and darted a glance at the fitting of one's dress, who has a right to suspect a virtue whose pins are so neatly attached? But a letter, a meager letter on diaphanous paper, scrawled in pretty handwriting as imperceptible as the feet of a humming-bird, is a sufficiently solid base for foolish indiscretions and impertinent pretentions.

And what does it matter whether or not the letter is signed? Not to sign it is a futile cowardice. Justice of God or malice of the devil, there is not a comma that does not accuse the hand that traced it. Poor women, you put into the most innocent phrase, written by your hand,

1 Barbey d'Aurevilly was born on 2 November, then recognized in French Catholicism, as it is today in Mexico, as "the day of the dead."

all the letters of your name. Oh well, that terrible slip in her system of conduct, Joséphine was on the point of risking. I even believe that she opened her writing-desk; but she closed it again with the fear of Pandora when she saw all the evils escaping from her open box; in her case, it was not hope that remained but reputation.

A voice had risen up in her soul: the voice of self-preservation, which had taken on the accent of the old Comtesse de Fiercy. "Make war," she said, "but never give hostages." *Oh, I was about to doom myself!* Joséphine exclaimed, but not in a manner to be heard—and that day, she went to bed with a shiver.

Do you know, Madame, what "doom myself" signified in the vocabulary of Joséphine's morality? Dooming oneself was the equivalent of not being able to find a husband Although one can still encounter those candid natures of honest men who marry, without being begged excessively, women of an extended epistolary reputation—or another—it is nevertheless a temerity to count on such good fortune, and a mind matured by experience refrains from seeing humanity too kindly.

Without that, Madame, we would have had one letter more! A letter like those I had the pleasure of reading, a few days ago, although they were addressed to someone more fortunate than me: a veritable model of civilization and aristocracy, in which the word amour had not been traced one single time, but in which there was mention of an irresistible nervous force to explain certain self-abandonments.

Women are such inexplicable beings; under the transparency of their skin and their gaze they hide such a mass of darkness that Josephine almost gave Aloys the cold shoulder the first time they met in society after his visit; but he, wanting to punish her for the contradictions of her chagrin, deployed such a vast magnificence of amiability that the sulk was soon vanquished. The smile returned to her lips; speech was never exiled therefrom for long. When he saw her as mild and smiling as usual, Aloys pirouetted on his heel and did not approach her again all evening.

She went all the colors of the rainbow, but darker. In fact, either that man was the devil in person, or he had borrowed his mocking manners from the demon. Oh, she thought, if she had him at her knees, what tears of vengeance she would have extracted from him, what cruel tears she would have made him shed! Yes, if she had him at her knees—but the difficulty was making him fall there.

In any case, Madame, if the angel with rosy cheeks that Shakespeare calls Patience abandoned that woman, whose blonde beauty was beginning to slip away a little, pale Vanity, who is not an angel, attached himself to her more strongly than ever. God is patient because he is eternal, say the Holy Books. She was not patient, because she was not eternal; so, while tearing the fingers of her gloves in chagrin and biting her lip a little harder, she said to herself proudly: *If I wanted, though . . .*! Then she stopped, terrified by the grandeur of her sacrifice; for it would have been necessary to expose her reputation— the most precious gem in a jewel-box that does not contain, it is true, all the diamonds of the crown—and she was still more preoccupied with a position than a vengeance.

A position—a marriage: identical ideas for a woman, since men wish it thus. Oh, don't blame her for that ambition, the only one you have left to women, men whose leonine egotism has taken everything! Since you buy with the best money in your pockets—or your soul—places, ranks, deputations, or a ministry, why forbid a woman the moral purchase of a husband, when the material purchase of one is impossible? Why forbid poor women that last resource, while awaiting their definitive emancipation, which cannot fail to arrive at the charming rate that we are going?

When, instead of modest, pure, retired, blushing lives in the holy shelter of the gynaeceum, they mingle with men, like female animals with quivering rumps, fuming nostrils and the appeals of a gross voluptuousness; when, ingrate toward God, who made them so beautiful and blinded them to their power, they prefer the vanity of writing to the substantial wealth of being loved, and soil their divine hands with ink in order to prove to their contemporaries the legitimacy of adultery!

But I believe that indignation is carrying me away. You are smiling, Madame, and I shall return to my story. In spite of the modern affectations of her language and her poses, Joséphine was only an affected woman and nothing more. She had the coquetries of a woman and the ambitions of a woman, but did she have the tenderness? Whatever the case might have been, and to remain truthful, she was only an innocent child, a perfection, a little girl of twelve years old who had just made her first communion that same morning, by comparison with some women I know, and whom men, as cowardly as they are imprudent, do not send away to make their compotes.

✳

Alas, Madame, that poor perfection was terribly embarrassed! She came and went between two thoughts: one of desire and the other of fear; she agitated between the fear of compromise and the desire to bend Aloys to her caprice; but it was impossible for her to remain for much longer in such a cruel fluctuation. It was a hammock for her reverie that was not silken, whose swinging did not produce sleep. That indecision became too violent. So vanity prevailed, and she ended up going all in.

✳

She played her final card—yes, Madame, intrepidly, like Masséna trapped in the peninsula on the Danube.[1] But before playing it, she put all the chances of success on her side, and one can say that her skill surpassed her bravery in a very feminine fashion; it was an indescribable tactic, a plan marvelously and subtly put together. There is no *Memoirs of Torcy* for such a politics.[2] If

---

1 In 1809 Napoléon's military commander André Masséna had to hold a position at Aspern, in order to enable the army to cross the Danube, for two days, under constant fierce attack.
2 The full title of the three-volume *Mémoires de M. de Torcy* –i.e,, Jean-Baptiste Colbert, Marquis de Torcy—continues "*pour server*

Joséphine had been able to write it—and perhaps the first woman who comes along will be able to repair that neglect quite well—we would have a treatise on *The Princess* by comparison with which that on *The Prince* would be a simple schoolboy exercise.

This, then, is what she imagined, that creature who was thought to be frivolous, with her vaporous airs, her vague gazes and her little cascades of words, which eddied in the ears of all those who had the patience to listen to them. She flirted and gossiped. She flirted and gossiped with all of us, with Aloys and with Monsieur Baudouin d'Artinel . . . and the time passed thus. And we strong minds, who imagine that we know everything about the inextricable nature of women, thought that Madame d'Alcy was, after all, only a flower-patterned doll mounted on a spring in order to slide more easily over the parquet of a salon.

Still waiting, still waiting, the month of August arrived. It is a month when the nights are so beautiful, so full of the balm of all the flowers, that even in the bosom of cities—those basins of marble filled with filth—the beautiful nights of August still have a charm and a perfume. The moon, that mild soul of the heavens, seems to

---

a l'histoire des negotiations" [to serve as a history of (diplomatic) negotiations].

spread more light then than in the other months of the year; she appears to cast a silvery foam upon all objects and to fringe them with a moist nacre.

✳

After half past eleven on one such night—had it been chosen by design?—the glazed door of a balcony on the Rue de Rivoli stood ajar. The balcony was deserted, but if one had had eyes sufficiently piercing to distinguish things through the glass, one would have seen two persons sitting side by side in an apartment that was almost obscure, where the dying lamp seemed, by means of its indecisive light, to want to level out all the weaknesses that it was destined to illuminate . . . for those two persons had their backs turned to the lamp. Were they two lovers, forgetting the world and life in some nonchalant reverie, full of smiles and kisses? The moon inclined her face curiously over the somber bushes of the Tuileries, as if her Endymion were in search of the mystery that night.

✳

It was a delectable night, with its sprinkling of stars—a night as ravishing as the faces of women that one has only seen once, perhaps in a dream, and who remain in our memories: one of those nights that one will not forget, if one has spent a little of it with God—or one's mistress, which is often the same thing, for only the

77

beloved face is worthy to gather the holy gleams that cause the imprint of kisses that remain on cheeks to sparkle . . . so brightly that one might think they were pearls or tears.

Tears that were not wept but which the mouth has poured in a soft intoxication—for in moments of happiness, as in those of agony, does not the blood of our hearts always find itself there? Oh, let us be happy very quickly! Let us hasten, fragile creatures that we are, let us hasten to resolve in a dew of kisses the flux of the heart that ought to rise higher than the mouth and drain away in bitter tears!

But it was not thus for them. It was Aloys and Joséphine who received, like a deluge of mortal emotions, the impressions of that evening of velvety light, repose and mystery . . .

He still had plenty of wit, wit enough to make Madame Joséphine believe that he was as calm as the sky and as chilly as the dew that was gliding over the windows. Only, by virtue of intimate suffering and the difficulty of suppressing his thought, that wit, ordinarily a flame so bright, with such ardent colors, only had sparse glimmers, like a few solitary bivouac fires on the edge of a nocturnal encampment.

He could take no more of a furious and bitter sensuality, and he was so close to her that he could feel the moisture of her shoulder against his. Oh, to remain thus forever, you who want to conserve unshaken your sage resolutions made that very morning! She had been rolling her *r*s, with a great deal of art and charm, all evening. She had even placed her hands on his with a perfectly played abandon, and for a man as purely amorous as Aloys she had done even more: two or three times, she had called him "Aloys."

As for sighs—those Galatean sighs that one represses and which one desires to be heard—and as for the gazes of a dying dove, she sowed them without counting them. That was the least she could do; so I shall not talk about it. And she went as far as a woman can go without being a Potiphar's wife who seizes the mantle in despair of the cause. And by the soul of my grandfather, she was pretty, in the half-light of the moon, a thousand times more so than in the false daylight of the candles by the light of which Aloys had contemplated her thus far.

And then, by hazard, caprice or a combination of the two, she had taken out her comb and her hair had fallen down her back. She resembled a Mary Magdalen—but no, though! She did not have such a tender or repentant attitude. Forgive my excessively vivid soul, abused young woman, pale privet whom Christ did not reject from his bosom before marching to execution, forgive me for comparing Joséphine to you! Canova's marble is more you than that daughter of society, for whom society had nothing to reproach, as to you. That marble expresses a hundred times more soul than Madame d'Alcy had.

But what would have been said that evening? Doubtless no one would have said it . . . no one except Aloys. O women, there are eagle eyes that you cannot puncture with your needles! Aloys' gaze revealed a profound passion, a formidable intoxication, but his smile was mocking—mocking with the mockery of Goethe when he wrote his most beautiful verses. Was it mocking her or him? He expended, in efforts and stifled desires, ten years of his life next to her. Did he like that cruel game? Is there a sensuality of torture as there is a sensuality of sensuality? Courageous young man, he had riposted with a *Madame* when she had called him *Aloys!*

"In spite of the charm of such a conversation," he said, getting to his feet—and he tottered—"I must ask you, Madame, for permission to retire."

"Already!" she cried—and she was truly emotional, for he remained the stronger and all those little expressions—a squandering of charming grimaces—had ended in a negative result by which she was internally humiliated.

"It will soon be midnight," said Aloys, looking at the clock. And he bowed, and went.

If that was a flight, Madame, admit that it as that of a Numidian![1] He went out with the satisfaction of male pride, a knotty stick torn from an oak on which one leans so nobly when one weakens. *That woman offered herself to me, and I didn't want to!*

Yes, she had offered herself . . . perhaps only to refuse herself, but she had offered—for there are certain mannerisms that have the significance of speech—like all those coquettes to the waist who love to make the poor devils who have the aberration of loving them suffer the torments of Tantalus. She remained motionless; when he had gone, her eyed fixed on the door, while a tear, colder than poison, ran down her still animated cheek: a tear of chagrin, of vanity, of anger, which dried up before reaching the mouth. Alas, if her mouth had drunk it, she might have found it so bitter that Joséphine might

---

1 The Roman historian Livy described the Numidian light cavalry, employed by Hannibal during the Second Punic War, as the best horsemen in the world. Their standard tactic of charging, hurling their javelins and then beating a rapid retreat to avoid counterattack was highly effective.

perhaps have been cured of the shameful dolor that had made it flow. Is it not said that one can cure the bite of a scorpion by crushing the wound?

※

The following day, she was more turbulent than ever at Madame de Dorff's house. I believe that she bit her lip harder when she perceived Aloys, but that was such a habitude in her that nothing could be induced from it. She spoke to him with a benevolence more marked than ever. In sum, she showed, in order to hide what she was experiencing, the marvelous elasticity that I had always supposed her to have: a celestial gift that has not been given to women in vain, and for which they ought to thank you on their knees every evening, O my God!

※

She quit the soirée early. We remarked that the honorable Monsieur d'Artinel did not take long to disappear over the horizon when her star had fled. It seemed that his jealousy—if there was jealousy in a chest much more exposed, it seemed, to asthma—had vanished a long time ago. Had Joséphine reassured him? But he had the ineffable delicacy of discretion, and we can only speak about our personal observation. "In any case," he said, taking his gummed cravat, "Monsieur Synarose has wit, but he spoils it by his conceit, and as fops go, those of my time were much more dangerous."

And after that judgment, worthy of a man accustomed to judging, he reposed majestically within himself—except when Joséphine was there. Then, he hastened toward her with the lightness of a zephyr, his phrases increasingly inflated by tears and interrupted by sighs. Isolation was killing him, that was certain, since the death of his wife, and he felt more keenly than ever than with a soul so full of sympathy, he had been created to live in company.

And then, he needed a governess for his daughters—a kind of mother who would teach them to stand upright and make a choice of novels for them. Already they were skirting the edge of adolescence, a difficult epoch to traverse. A lover might arrive some day or other, and it would be necessary to teach them the attitude that well-brought-up young women ought to adopt at the first declaration.

※

And all those considerations doubtless irritated the already-sharp taste that Monsieur d'Artinel had for Joséphine. She, who spoke about virtue, would make his daughters love it. They would love it to the point of not preferring anyone. Shrewd people therefore calculated that Monsieur Baudouin d'Artinel was approaching a second marriage, in proportion to his regret for the first.

I was one of the last to leave Madame de Dorff's that evening. She lived on the Rue de Castiglione, and I returned home thoughtfully, like a losing gambler—for I had played and lost—via the Rue de Rivoli. There was a moonlight of great amiability for tutors, husbands, thieves, poets and other persons interested in nocturnal observation. It was a transparent and sonorous night, although silent—the understudy of the previous night.

Is that a thief or are we in Spain? I asked myself, as I aimed my lorgnette at a kind of body suspended between the sky and the pavement. I looked harder; I looked again. A woman was leaning timidly over the edge of the balcony and designing the most gracious curve against the azure of the sky. It was not a charming scene of farewell, as you have shown us, O Shakespeare, but rather that which had to precede it. And frankly, whether illusion or favorable perspective, the leaning woman, O Shakespeare, was as pretty as Juliet!

Your Juliet! That amour of my first dreams that sweet and yet terrestrial creature, passionate like us in a body more divine than a soul—poor timid and bold child!— clad only in the jasmine of the balcony, in the midst of which she appears in a nudity more chaste than that of the sky devoid of its clouds, than that of the dawn which is beginning to break—for the dawn knows that she is nude and blushes . . . but Juliet had forgotten.

But Romeo? Was that your Romeo, O my great Shakespeare? Or was it a cruel parody of him? Ah, handsome Montague, it was you, Monsieur d'Artinel. I recognized you very well with your slightly rounded back—but Plato had high shoulders, and was he not a trifle hunchbacked? In mounting the poetic ladder of green silk, you had precious elegance, suppleness, agility and grace! How well your gravity suits you, perched in mid-air! Oh, poor mortals that we are, having past fifty years, and then going to judge, after that?

And he arrived at the balcony without encumbrance. Now, I ought to confess here, Madame, that I did not see or hear any of what followed. The glazed door closed on the happy couple . . . and the moon was still hastening through the tranquil sky. She was not blushing, that impudent moon, and I, who had stopped to gaze at that singular scene, did as she did and went to bed.

The rest . . . is an impenetrable mystery sealed by the seven seals of the Eternal. My story could, Madame, finish at that glazed door; it would gain a poetic vagueness there that would suit it, an immaterial aureole. But I detest poets, their lies and their reticences. I hate them for many reasons, but above all because they spoil life for us in such a way that it no longer resembles, for us, anything but a courtesan, when our first amour has flown.

I shall not finish my story like a poet, then, Madame, but I shall rather make you drink from the chalice of reality, all the way to the dregs. The dregs, Madame, were the marriage of Monsieur d'Artinel and Joséphine, which took place a few days later at the Assumption. We saw her playing fortunate modesty there, under her bridal veil, and becoming Madame d'Artinel. It was a lovely spectacle. Doubtless she had made the honorable and delicate Monsieur Baudouin d'Artinel understand that a dazzling official reparation was necessary for the damage that an enthusiasm of the heart and a Spanish balcony scene had done to her reputation, the wealth that she preferred, after all, to everything else.

And that, said in a voice full of tears, in a premiere performance voice, had not failed to stir the soul of the sensitive counselor. In any case, he must have been proud of the preference that she confessed, and which she had proven in such a romantic fashion. All things considered, he was a man of generous nature and a woman compromised by him, that rare thing nowadays—not compromised women but Monsieur Baudouin d'Artinel's manner of treating them—seemed to him to be a sacred object. In any case, she had always pleased him . . . and it is thus that, after assembling all his reasons for being the happiest of men, he became the man in question by marrying her.

It was on a Saturday that he married her. The little church of the Assumption was full—the ravishing church that expresses verity in art with so much eloquence, and which, by virtue of that fact, was, believe me, well worthy of covering the verity of the sentiments that Joséphine then expressed . . . but a nuance of embarrassment is not unbefitting a woman on such a day She no longer had the scarlet cheeks that she had always had when leaving Madame de Dorff's house, but it is true that she did not say anything. She was as pale as Aloys ordinarily was—Aloys, whom she had perceived in the chapel, and who had lost his own habitual pallor; for he had got rid of his gastritis, which had perhaps not gone far and had reentered his life—but who can tell whether it had ever really left?—by way of lobster lunches abundantly washed down by Bordeaux.

It had reentered that life, which the spiritualists of our era disdain and the women of pure ether who faint on reading Joubert,[1] but which, after all, is the true life for those who believe that the scorn of sensation is a parricide for thought. Like Sheridan, the immortal spirit, he found that getting drunk was an agreeable thing when the heart made one feel ill.

Even at the strongest point of his love for Joséphine he haunted the Café Anglais. I had often seen him there, exhausted by those mute crises of great hearts— invisible bullfights—raising his spirits with his glass and seeking forgetfulness therein, between intoxication and irony: two very sad clowns, born on the same night of Despair.

On the eve of Joséphine's marriage, rumor said—but who can believe rumor?—that he had been seen supping tête-à-tête with a woman who was not Madame d'Alcy. Madame d'Alcy was an angel whom any supper naturally caused horror; for at dessert a woman is true, and for modesties like Joséphine's, to be true is almost to be naked. In any case, on that day she no longer belonged

1 Joseph Joubert (1754-1824) achieved a posthumous celebrity in 1838 when Chateaubriand published numerous excerpts from his letters and notebooks, revealing a preoccupation with his continual poor health—which, he asserted, gave a certain valuable subtlety to his soul.

to herself. She had signed the bail of her happiness that very morning, and in the evening, gave all the customary caresses of stepmothers to the little d'Artinels.

It was not, therefore, Joséphine. But in that case, who the devil was it? Rumor added—but rumor is such a liar!—that Aloys' female partner, at that supper, bizarre to say the least, did not resemble Madame d'Alcy at all. She had not, of necessity, that perfume of aristocratic virtue; she was not an angel from the same heaven. She was an inferior being—charming, unfortunately—worthy of the scorn of all women; a species of tigress . . . for appetite only . . . who ate with beautiful nacreous teeth, and who, her corset full of the burning marble of youth, found herself sufficiently different from a sylphide to prefer a glass of champagne to the dew in flowers. Let us not believe rumor, Madame. It has said . . . what has it not said? Personally, I don't know what people do at those funeral repasts given before the last supper of amour, but what I do know is that the following day, at the Assumption, Aloys had all the appropriate gravity— which is to say that he was cheerful.

As for Monsieur d'Artinel, he was serious and irreproachable. He was wearing the customary costume: a magnificent blue coat, the second coat of that color that he had ever worn, since his first marriage, for it is necessary to marry in blue if one wants the union to be happy. In that we differ from the Orientals, for whom blue is a sign of mourning; they wear it when they weep, and we when we marry—which proves, philosophers say, the unity of the human mind.

With the indispensable blue suit he had also bought the requisite ring: the ring that is called so singularly an *alliance*, and is the first link in a chain that has no end. That ring was a true masterpiece. The names of Monsieur Baudouin d'Artinel and Joséphine were mingled there with mysterious dates, so well that the devil himself would not have been able to disentangle them. When the circle was passed over Joséphine's slender finger, Aloys, who was watching the symbolic ceremony very attentively, leaned toward me and said: "Do you remember Hannibal's ring?"

Is he mad? I thought. *Or has amour, so rich in unexpected developments, thrown him into historical studies?* But he did not notice my astonishment, or, if he saw it, it did not stop him.

"Hannibal's ring," he went on, "had a stone, and under that stone there was a drop of poison. It was with that drop of poison that Hannibal killed himself.[1] Well,

---

1 The allegation that the Carthaginian general Hannibal Barca died after swallowing poion contained in a ring, made by Juvenal, contradicts an assertion made by Pausanius that he died of a fever

there are rings without stones that contain a poison more subtle than Hannibal's, because it's an invisible poison. Only,"—he added, with perfect gaiety—"that poison doesn't kill great men but something very tiny: it kills amour."

"I give you my compliment," I said to him. He saw that I had understood, and did not reject the compliment. "Yes, you're right," I went on, "we all have our Hannibal's rings in life, but that one is one of the strangest, because it isn't on our fingers that we wear the rings that poison us."[1]

---

caused by an infected wound. Even the year of his death was uncertain, various Roman historians offering three different estimations. The story of the ring naturally exercised much greater appeal to later imaginations than the alternative.

1 This assertion is deliberately vague, and contemporary readers would have been free to read what they liked into it, as are modern ones. It is worth noting, however, that "la bague d'Annibal" might have resonated in the mind of the author, and those of contemporary readers, with the phrase "la bague de Hans Carvel," ultimately derived from a story first committed to print in a collection of fifteenth-century lewd tales, *Liber Facietarum*, by Poggio Bracciolini, which was recycled by Rabelais and than rendered even more familiar in France by "L'Anneau de Hans Carvel," one of Jean de la Fontaine's fables in verse. Carvel, an old doctor with a young wife, dreams that the devil gives him a ring, promising that it will prevent him from being cuckolded as long as he wears it. When he wakes up, he finds that his finger is stuck in his wife's vagina—with the result that "l'anneau de Hans Carvel" and "la bague de Hans Carvel" became common euphemisms for that anatomical feature

Joséphine has, therefore, a position in society, as well as a husband and three beautiful young girls as meek as Madame Deshoulières' sheep,[1] to torment—which is, it must be agreed, an agreeable pastime when one is bored. The habitude remains of being amiable with her husband. She still talks about virtue with the same abundance, and she is not known to have a lover as yet.

I would wager that she does not have one. However, with the young women who have husbands or lovers as young as themselves, she confesses that she only has esteem for Monsieur d'Artinel, and that she only married him out of pity. Does she regret Aloys? I forgot to tell you, Madame, that Aloys went to her wedding ball, as he had gone to her wedding mass, and that he had asked her for the honor of the first quadrille, since Monsieur d'Artinel did not dance. That day he had doubtless swallowed the toad that Chamfort[2] counsels swallowing every morning before leaving home, in order to be a man of the world.

---

1 The reference is to the famous pastoral idyll "Le Moutons" (1688) by Antoinette Deshoulières.
2 The writer Nicolas Chamfort (1741-1794), famous for his sarcastic wit; he was secretary to several members of Louis XVI's court before becoming an ardent Jacobin. His attempted suicide in 1793, when under threat of arrest for being too moderate a Jacobin, added to his legend: having bungled a pistol-shot to the head and only smashed his nose, he stabbed himself repeatedly with a paper-knife, but fell unconscious, was revived and survived for seven months in police custody, reportedly in terrible agony.

www.ingramcontent.com/pod-product-compliance
Lightning Source LLC
Chambersburg PA
CBHW050156110726
47898CB00008B/2825